There Was a Man and He Was Mad

Adapted by John M. Feierabend

Illustrated by Aaron Joshua

GIA Publications, Inc.
Chicago

To my Mom, Dennis, Doug, Bill and everyone who believed in me.
– Aaron Joshua

There Was a Man and He Was Mad

This old nonsense song has been enjoyed for generations and exists in many variations. This song can be found in James Orchard Halliwell's "The Nursery Rhymes of England" in 1886 and in Mary O. Eddy's "Ballads and Songs from Ohio" published in 1939.

"There Was a Man and He Was Mad" was also enjoyed and shared by one of the most famous families of American folk music, the Seegers. In 1948, Ruth Crawford Seeger included a variation of it in her book *American Folk Songs for Children*. Later, her children Mike and Peggy were recorded taking turns improvising rhyming verses. Their brother Pete also recorded and sang this song in concerts, where he would invite the audience to join in singing the last word of each verse.

The melody of this song is very simple and therefore easy to learn, and is reminiscent of the favorite children's folk song, "Old McDonald."

Throughout its aural life, "There Was a Man and He Was Mad" continued to be shared for no other apparent reason than for the pleasure of placing this man in ridiculous situations.

This book captures one of the many wonderful versions of the song, beautifully illustrated by Aaron Joshua, who adds a new twist to the story. Perhaps you will be inspired to join in and contribute to the life of this song by creating new comical situations for our mad man to experience!

— John M. Feierabend

Download an mp3 recording of this song at no cost at www.giamusic.com/twam

G-7179
ISBN: 978-1-57999-681-9.
Printed in China by RR Donnelley in November 2021

7404 S. Mason Ave.
Chicago, IL 60638
www.giamusic.com

here was a man and he was mad,

so he jumped into a paper bag.

But the paper bag, it was so thin,

that he jumped onto the tip of a pin.

The tip of the pin was very sharp.

so he jumped onto an Irish harp.

But the Irish harp
was very pretty,

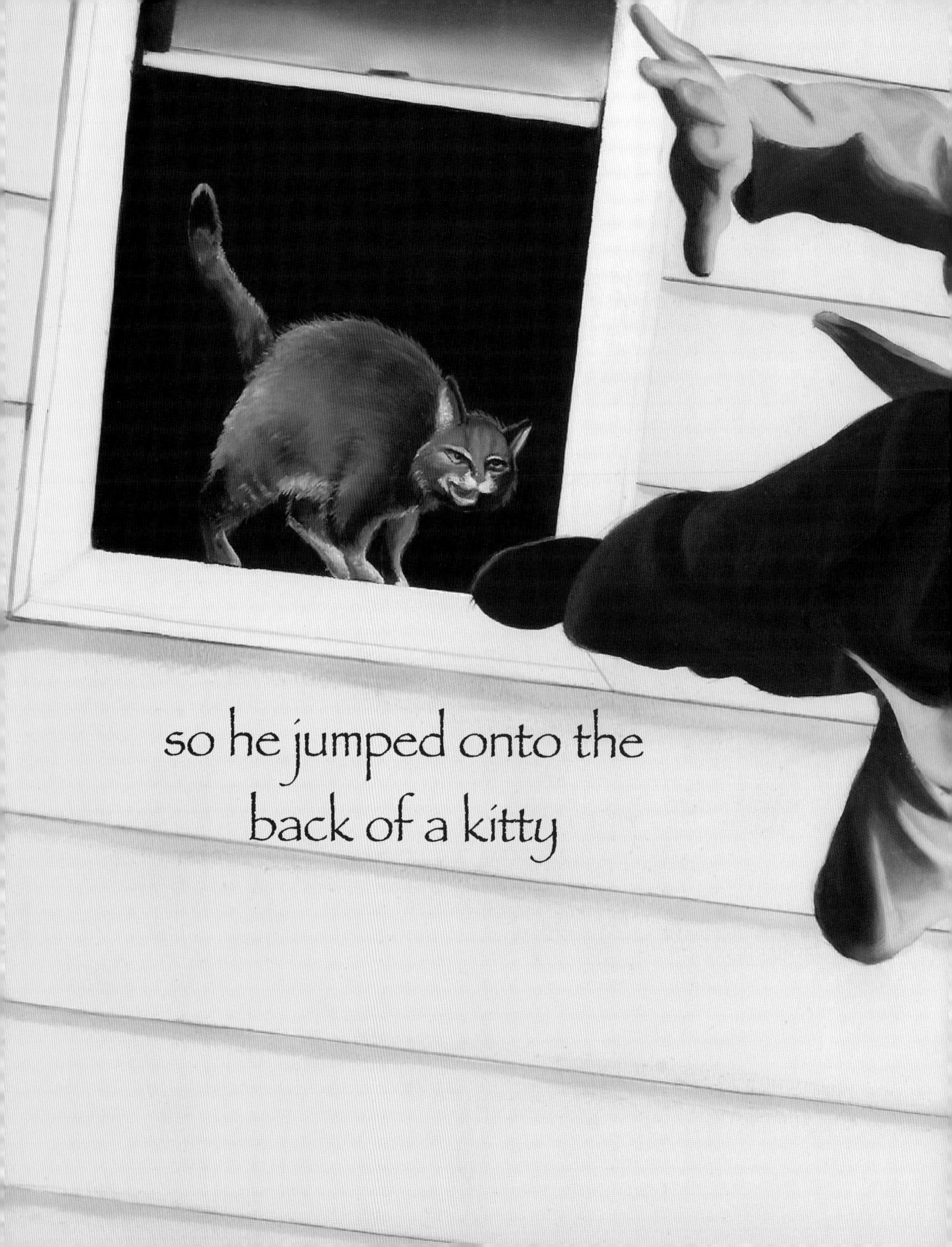

so he jumped onto the
back of a kitty

The little kitty
began to scratch,

so he jumped into a cabbage patch.

But the cabbage patch
was way too big,

so he jumped onto the
back of a pig.

The little pig began to tickle,

so he jumped onto a big dill pickle.

But the big dill
pickle was oh,
so sour,

so he jumped onto a big sun flower.

Then along came
a bee

and stung him on the chin,

and that was the end of him.

There was a man and he was mad. (song)

Additional Verses

2. But the paper bag, it was so thin, that he jumped onto the tip of a pin.

3. But the tip of the pin was very sharp, so he jumped onto an Irish harp.

4. But the Irish harp was very pretty, so he jumped onto the back of a kitty.

5. But the little kitty began to scratch, so he jumped into a cabbage patch.

6. But the cabbage patch was way too big, so he jumped onto the back of a pig.

7. But the little pig began to tickle, so he jumped onto a big dill pickle.

8. But that dill pickle was oh, so sour, so he jumped onto a big sun flower.

9. Then along came a bee and stung him on the chin, and that was the end of him.

Download an mp3 recording of this song at no cost at www.giamusic.com/twam